Beautiful
Blue Eyes

WRITTEN AND ILLUSTRATED BY

Marianne Richmond

sourcebooks
jabberwocky

Beautiful Blue Eyes

Published by Sourcebooks Jabberwocky,
an imprint of Sourcebooks, Inc.
P.O. Box 4410, Naperville, Illinois 60567-4410
(630) 961-3900
Fax: (630) 961-2168
www.jabberwockykids.com

Library of Congress Cataloging-in-Publication data
is on file with the publisher.

Source of Production: Leo Paper, Heshan City,
Guangdong Province, China
Date of Production: January 2011
Run Number: 14147

Printed and bound in China.
LEO 10 9 8 7 6 5 4 3 2 1

Also available from author & illustrator
Marianne Richmond:

The Gift of an Angel
The Gift of a Memory
Hooray for You!
The Gifts of Being Grand
I Love You So...
Dear Daughter
Dear Son
Dear Granddaughter
Dear Grandson
Dear Mom
My Shoes Take Me Where I Want to Go
Fish Kisses and Gorilla Hugs
Happy Birthday to You!
I Love You So Much...
You Are My Wish Come True
Big Sister
Big Brother
If I Could Keep You Little
The Night Night Book
Beautiful Brown Eyes
I Wished for You, an adoption story

Beautiful
Blue Eyes

is dedicated to Julia,
my blue-eyed girl.

When you were little,
I looked into your eyes,
knowing their **color**
would be a **surprise.**

Would they
be **brown** as a mountain
or **green** like the earth?

Would they start as one color
and **change** after birth?

I watched and I waited
    as your eyes chose their hue,
deciding in time
    on their **beautiful blue**.

Blue as a **butterfly**

or the **sparkling sea.**

Blue as the **bluebird**
who sings
in her tree.

Pretty, for sure,
those **"blues"** I know,
and, oh, what they tell me
about you as you grow.

"*Eyes cannot talk!*"
you say to me.
"*Mouths are for talking.*
Eyes are to see!"

You're right, you know, without a doubt.
I see **in**, and you see **out.**

But while I'm looking, guess what I SEE?
I see your eyes **speaking** to me.

They tell me **so** much
of what you're about—
Your **heart** within,
your **self** throughout.

Your **thoughts** and **ways**
and **moods** each one.
Some up, some down,
some blah, some fun.

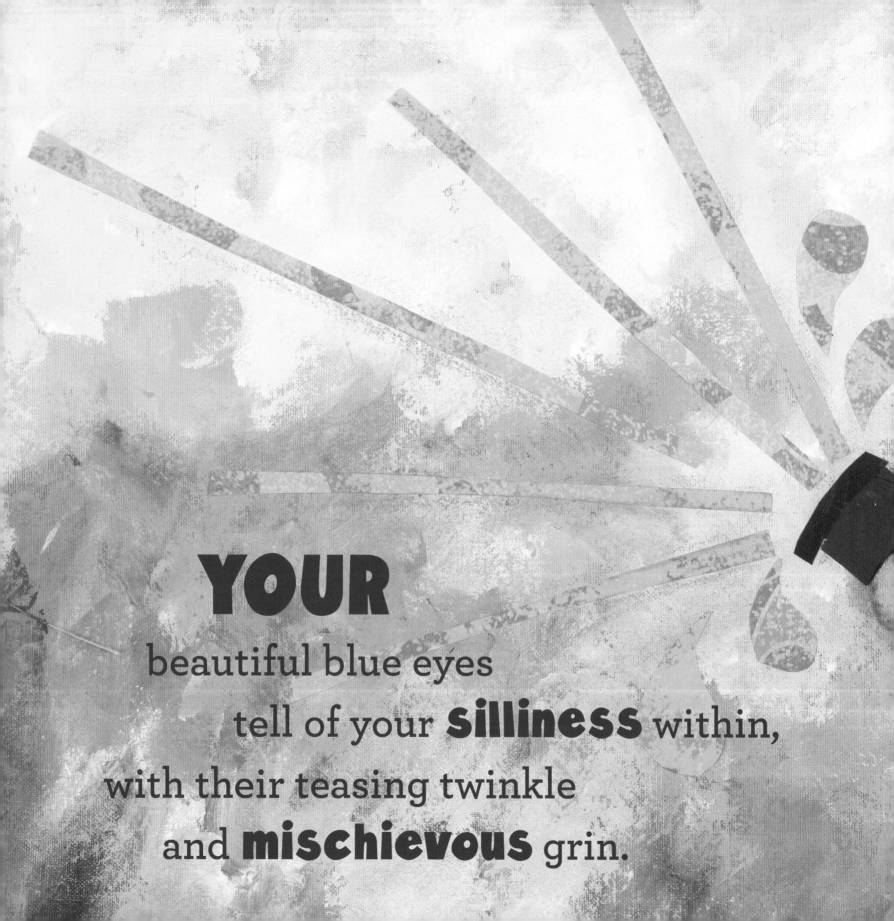

YOUR

beautiful blue eyes

tell of your **silliness** within,

with their teasing twinkle

and **mischievous** grin.

They show me your **originality** when you're with a friend, playing and **pretending** from sun up to day's end.

YOUR

beautiful blue eyes

tell of **thoughtfulness** too,

when you show care for others

by the **kind deeds** you do.

"How about when I'm **sick**?" you ask.
"*Do my eyes show* **sorry** *or* **sad**?
Do they tell you when I'm **gloomy**,
and when I'm just plain **mad**?"

Yes, all those and more,
your beautiful **blues** say,
telling me in a look
what your voice may
never say.

YOUR

beautiful blue eyes
show a **stubbornness** too,
when you just won't agree
to what you should do!

They tell me of your **curiosity** in the things you want to know.

"Where do freckles come from?"

"How tall can giraffes grow?"

And when tears fall down,
your **blues** tell too,
of **disappointment** or **worry**
about some thing or some who.

"My eyes talk **a lot**," you say,
"without me knowing
all the feelings
they can be showing."

Even **more** too,
they reveal your **affection**.
They show **sweetness** and **joy**
when you share
your **attention**.

Two of my favorite eyes, still,
(*though you may not agree*)
tell me of **sleepiness**
as they blink next to me.

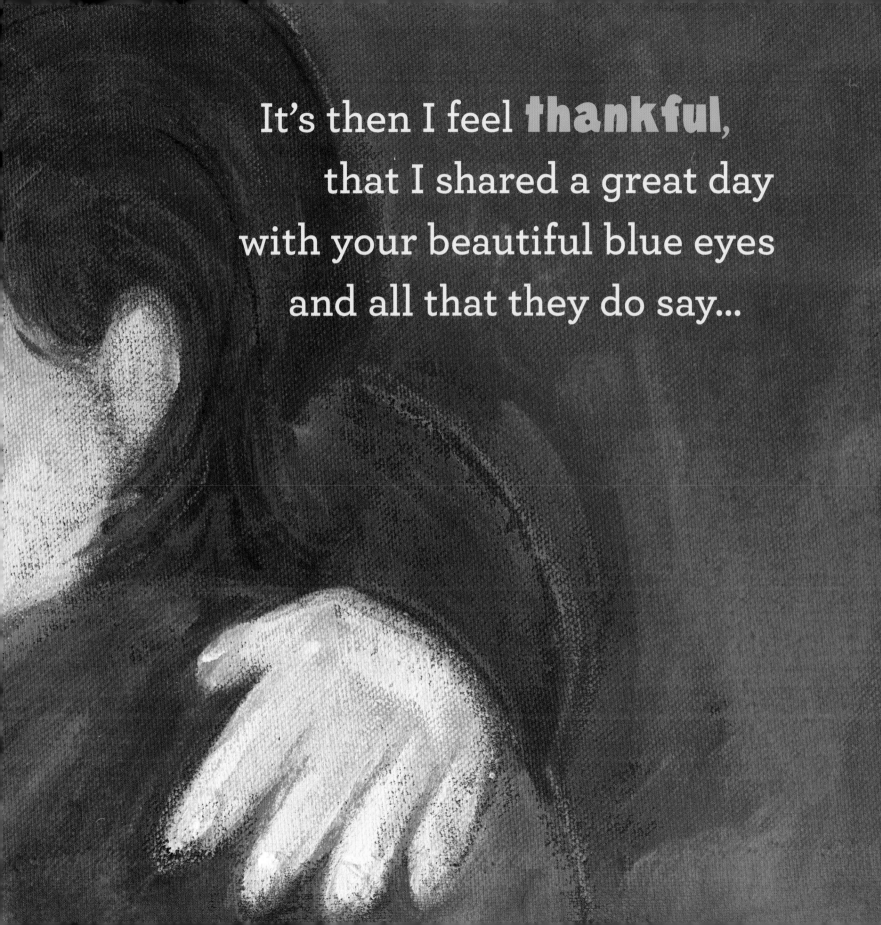

It's then I feel **thankful**,
that I shared a great day
with your beautiful blue eyes
and all that they do say...